REALLY STRANGE ADAPTATIONS

REALLY STRANGE

AMPHIBIANS

MELISSA RAÉ SHOFNER

PowerKiDS press
New York

Published in 2017 by The Rosen Publishing Group, Inc.
29 East 21st Street, New York, NY 10010

First Edition

Editor: Theresa Morlock
Book Design: Reann Nye

Photo Credits: Cover, p. 1 (amphibian) Paul Starosta/Corbis Documentary/Getty Images; cover, pp. 1–32 (background) Kichigin/Shutterstock.com; pp. 4, 11 (all) Dirk Ercken/Shutterstock.com; p. 5 davemhuntphotography/Shutterstock.com; p. 6 Eric Isselee/Shutterstock.com; p. 7 Ch'ien Lee/ Minden Pictures/Getty Images; p. 8 Jason Patrick Ross/Shutterstock.com; p. 9 https://commons.wikimedia.org/wiki/File:Ranapipiensmoulting.jpg; pp. 10, 30 (caecilian) reptiles4all/Shutterstock.com; p. 13 Randimal/Shutterstock.com; p. 14 Paul Starosta/Corbis Documentary/Getty Images; p. 15 Westend61/Getty Images; p. 16 Pedro H. Bernardo/Moment/Getty Images; p. 17 Joel Sartore/ National Geographic/Getty Images; p. 18 Konrad Wothe/Minden Pictures/ Getty Images; p. 19 Aleksey Stemmer/Shutterstock.com; p. 20 Buzz Photos/Shutterstock.com; p. 21 David A. Northcott/Corbis Documentary/Getty Images; p. 22 Anneka/Shutterstock.com; p. 23 Mark Moffett/Minden Pictures/Getty Images; p. 25 Stephen Dalton/Minden Pictures/ Getty Images; p. 26 D. Parer & E. Parer-Cook/Minden Pictures/Getty Images; p. 27 https://commons.wikimedia.org/wiki/File:Lithobates_sylvaticus_(Woodfrog).jpg; p. 29 Bildagentur Zoonar GmbH/ Shutterstock.com; p. 30 (glass frog) Pete Oxford/Minden Pictures/Getty Images; p. 30 (chinese giant salamander) TOM MCHUGH/Science Source/Getty Images; p. 30 (frog eating insect) Dr. Morley Read/ Shutterstock.com.

Cataloging-in-Publication Data

Names: Shofner, Melissa Raé.
Title: Really strange amphibians / Melissa Raé Shofner.
Description: New York : PowerKids Press, 2017. | Series: Really strange adaptations | Includes index.
Identifiers: ISBN 9781499427400 (pbk.) | ISBN 9781499428582 (library bound) | ISBN 9781508152972 (6 pack)
Subjects: LCSH: Amphibians–Juvenile literature.
Classification: LCC QL644.2 S56 2017 | DDC 597.8–dc23

Manufactured in the United States of America

CPSIA Compliance Information: Batch #BW17PK: For Further Information contact Rosen Publishing, New York, New York at 1-800-237-9932

CONTENTS

AWESOME AMPHIBIANS 4
ON THE MOVE 6
STRANGE SKIN 8
A COLORFUL WARNING 10
TINY TOXIC NEWTS 12
HAIRY HORRORS 14
CAECILIANS 16
LAYING EGGS 18
SURINAM TOADS 20
LET'S EAT! 22
MAGICAL AXOLOTLS 24
HARSH HABITATS 26
FRIGHTENING FUNGUS 28
GLOSSARY 31
INDEX 32
WEBSITES 32

AWESOME AMPHIBIANS

Amphibians are animals that live part of their lives in water and part of their lives on land. In fact, "amphibian" is a Greek word that means "of both kinds of life." There are three main groups: frogs and toads, newts and salamanders, and caecilians.

There are about 7,000 known species of amphibians on Earth. They're found on every continent except Antarctica. They live in many different **habitats**, including wetlands, mountains, and rain forests. You can find amphibians beneath logs and rocks, in the water,

Crested newts have learned to play dead if they sense danger. If predators don't lose interest, the newts release a bad-tasting, foul-smelling **toxin**.

underground, and even in trees. Most prefer warm, wet climates. However, some live in much drier places.

Amphibians are very sensitive to changes in the **environment**. They've had to adapt in order to survive. Read on to learn more about the strangest amphibian **adaptations**.

MASTER OF DISGUISE

The Vietnamese mossy frog gets its name from the bumps and colors on its skin. It looks just like moss! This frog blends in with its surroundings, which is an adaptation called camouflage. When startled, the mossy frog tucks in its limbs and holds very still so that it can't be seen. This adaptation protects it from predators. No two mossy frogs look exactly the same.

ON THE MOVE

Metamorphosis refers to the changes in form that frogs go through. Most amphibians go through metamorphosis of some kind. Most frogs lay their eggs in water. When the eggs hatch, the young tadpoles begin swimming around right away. Their tail helps them move swiftly through the water. At the next stage, froglets begin growing legs and losing their tail. Soon the frogs are ready for life on land.

Some adult amphibians that spend time swimming have webbed feet. This adaptation helps their feet work like paddles to move them easily through the water.

FLYING FROGS!

Wallace's flying frogs live in the jungle trees of Malaysia and Borneo. They have a special adaptation to help them "fly" from tree to tree when hunting or feeling threatened—extra skin between their toes and on their sides. When they take a leap, they spread out their toes, and the extra skin catches the air as they fall. They sometimes glide for more than 50 feet (15 m). Large toe pads help them land gently.

Frogs and toads are often seen hopping around. Some can leap more than 30 times the length of their body. Others, such as the banded rubber frog, prefer to walk. The waxy tree frog lives in trees in Central and South America. It uses its long legs and **opposable** thumbs to slowly reach and step from branch to branch.

STRANGE SKIN

Some salamanders breathe entirely through their skin. This dusky salamander doesn't have lungs at all.

If you've ever held a frog or a salamander, it might have felt slippery and slimy. Their moist skin allows oxygen from water or air to pass through. That's right, amphibians actually breathe through their skin! To keep their skin from drying out, they often live in damp climates or near ponds and streams.

Batrachologists, or scientists who study amphibians, are studying some amphibian adaptations to see if they can be useful to humans. For example, frogs have substances on their skin that protect them from germs. Scientists think these substances might be able to fight illnesses. Scientists are also studying frogs in Australia that produce chemicals in their skin that keep away bugs. Depending on what a frog eats, the chemicals can smell like nuts, herbs, or rotting flesh.

EAT WHAT YOU SHED

Toads, frogs, and some salamanders shed their skin regularly. Fresh, new skin is revealed when the old skin falls off. Scientists think this may be an adaptation that keeps the skin soft so oxygen can pass through it. After they shed, amphibians will eat their old skin. Gross! The old skin has important **nutrients** that amphibians need to stay healthy. They may also eat their old skin so that predators won't know they were there.

A COLORFUL WARNING

Poison dart (or arrow) frogs are some of the prettiest creatures on Earth. They have bright colors and bold patterns that warn predators to stay away. Some of these frogs can be deadly. Others aren't as harmful, but their colors still make predators think twice before moving in for a meal.

There are more than 100 species of poison dart frogs. The golden poison arrow frog is one of the largest at about 2 inches (5 cm) long. One of these little frogs has enough toxin in its skin to kill 10 adult men.

Interestingly, poison dart frogs raised in **captivity** don't develop toxins. Scientists think the frogs get their toxins from insects they eat in their natural habitat. The insects feed on poisonous plants.

Scientists are trying to use toxins from poison dart frogs to create new medications for humans.

TINY TOXIC NEWTS

Rough-skinned newts are cute little creatures, measuring only 2.5 to 3.5 inches (6.4 to 8.9 cm) long. Don't let their small size fool you, though. These tiny newts produce a harmful substance called tetrodotoxin (TTX) in their skin. TTX blocks communication between the brain and the rest of the body. Victims lose feeling, become dizzy and shaky, and finally lose the ability to move. TTX is often deadly.

When threatened, rough-skinned newts lift their head and flash their bright underside as a warning. Most predators get the hint, but some garter snakes aren't afraid. They're immune to TTX, which means eating a newt won't kill them. Rough-skinned newts are adapting and becoming more toxic. However, garter snakes are adapting, too, by becoming more resistant to TTX.

Rough-skinned newts have enough TTX in their skin to kill 25,000 mice. Since there's no known cure for their poison, they're dangerous to people as well. This adaptation protects them from most predators.

HAIRY HORRORS

Have you ever seen a frog with hair? The hairy frog lives in the jungles and forests of central Africa. It gets its name from the "hairs" that sometimes run down the sides and back legs of adult males of the species. Scientists believe these hairs work like gills on the outside of the frog's body. They may be an adaptation to help the frogs get more oxygen because their lungs are very small.

Some people in Africa eat hairy frogs. They hunt using spears so the frogs don't stab them.

BROKEN BONES

The Spanish ribbed newt also uses its own bones as weapons. When the newt feels threatened, it will first produce a toxin in its skin. If that doesn't work, the newt will turn its ribs forward. The sharp ends of the rib bones break through the skin. As they poke through, the ribs become covered with the toxin. A predator will get a mouthful of bad-tasting spines if it tries to eat the newt now.

Hairy frogs are also called "horror frogs." This nickname comes from a strange adaptation these frogs have for protection. When attacked, a hairy frog will break its own toes and force the snapped bones through its skin to use like claws. The "claws" later **retract**, and the bones and skin begin to heal.

CAECILIANS

When people talk about amphibians, it's rare for them to mention caecilians. These wormlike creatures aren't often seen. They spend much of their time underground or underwater.

THANKS MOM!

Caecilians have an unusual way of caring for their young. In some species, a mother will lay eggs and protect them until they hatch. Once they hatch, baby caecilians use their teeth to scrape off and eat a special layer of their mother's outer skin. In other species, the eggs will hatch inside the mother caecilian. The babies will eat special tissue that grows inside their mother until they are big enough to be born.

Scientists still have much to learn about these mysterious amphibians.

Although some live in the water, caecilians have adapted to life underground. Some species don't have eyes, while others have eyes that are covered with skin or bone. They don't need to see well because it's dark underground. They have special **tentacles** on their faces to help them find prey and explore their environment. Caecilians move around like worms and have hard skulls for digging tunnels. Their strong jaws have two sets of muscles to keep their mouth closed tight when tunneling. They have dozens of needle-sharp teeth.

LAYING EGGS

Some amphibians go to great lengths to make sure their offspring have a good chance at survival. Strawberry poison dart frogs, for example, don't lay their eggs in a body of water where they could be eaten by predators. Instead, they lay their eggs on land. When the eggs hatch, the mother carries the tadpoles on her back. She puts them inside large tropical flowers that collect water. She returns regularly to lay eggs into the plants for the tadpoles to eat.

The waxy tree frog doesn't hop. To build a nest, it must climb up a tree by using its feet.

The waxy tree frog builds a leaf nest that hangs over a body of water and then lays its eggs in the nest. When the eggs hatch, the tadpoles fall into the water below. They live in the water until they develop into frogs.

SURINAM TOADS

Surinam toads live in the rain forests of South America. They spend most of their time in muddy rivers. It can be hard to see in the dirty water, but they've adapted to these conditions. Surinam toads have long toes with very sensitive tips that help them detect nearby prey. These toads don't have teeth or a tongue. When they catch a meal, they swallow it whole.

Surinam toads have great camouflage. Their rough, brown skin and flat body makes them look just like the rocks and leaves in their habitat.

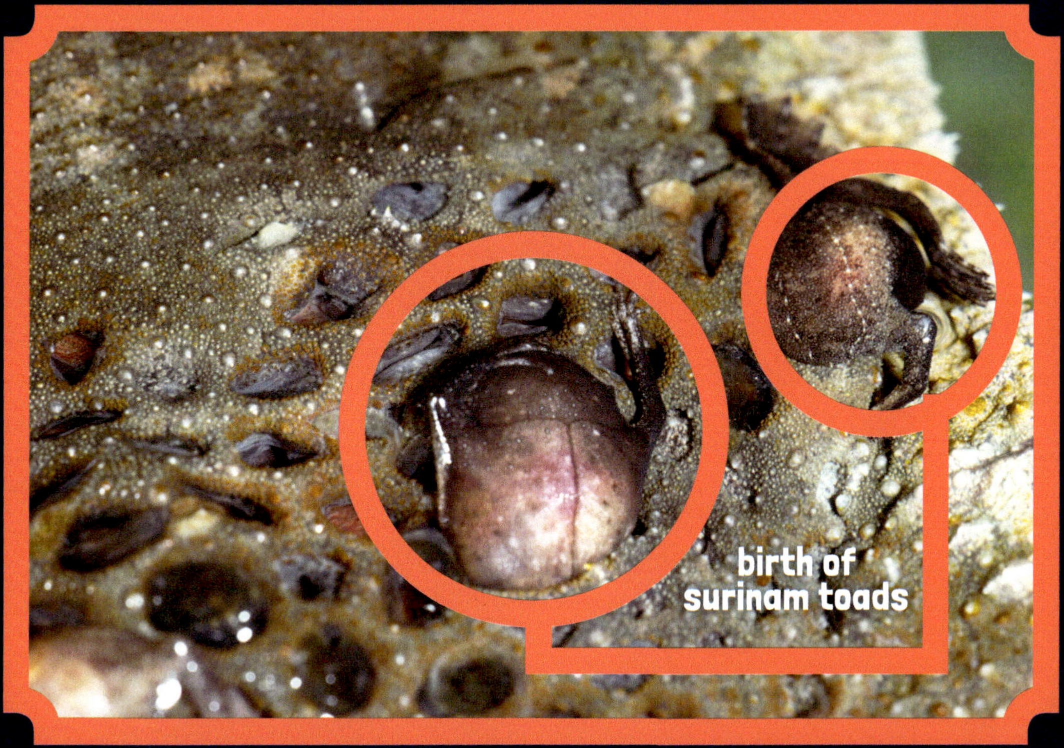

The strangest adaptation of Surinam toads is the way they care for their young. The male toad pushes the eggs onto a mother toad's back, and skin grows over them. The eggs hatch, but the babies stay put for a few months and continue to grow. When they're ready, the little toads break through the skin on their mother's back.

LET'S EAT!

Some amphibians have special adaptations to help them eat. Ornate horned frogs have a huge mouth that appears to stretch across their entire front half. They wait until prey wanders by, then they attack and swallow their meal whole. Ornate horned frogs will eat pretty much anything that fits in their mouth. Sometimes they try to eat something too big and end up choking.

A small frog in Brazil called *Xenohyla truncata* jumps with its mouth open toward fruit hanging in trees. It's the only frog species that eats fruit.

The now-**extinct** gastric brooding frog actually had to stop eating for a period of time. A female would swallow her own eggs and let them hatch and grow inside her stomach. Her stomach would stop working for about 40 days. The mother frog wouldn't eat again until after her babies crawled out of her mouth.

MAGICAL AXOLOTLS

Axolotls are a group of salamanders native to two lakes in Mexico. Unfortunately one of the lakes has dried up, leaving the axolotls with a lot less natural habitat. They're considered an **endangered** species. However, they're adapting to their changing lifestyle in the wild and also making a comeback in captivity.

One adaptation that helps axolotls survive is called neoteny. In axolotls, neoteny means they can reproduce without undergoing metamorphosis. Axolotls grow bigger, but don't mature. They keep their tail and feathery gills so they can continue to live in the water. Since they don't make the full change into adult salamanders, axolotls are able to reproduce much sooner. This allows them to quickly increase their populations in the wild.

GROWING NEW PARTS

Axolotls have another incredible adaptation that helps them survive. Like other salamanders, they can regenerate, or regrow, most of their body parts if they become injured. This neat trick isn't limited to just their limbs or tail. They can also regrow parts of their eyes, jaw, spine, and major organs, including their brain. Scientists are studying axolotls in hopes of learning more about regeneration and other healing techniques that may someday be used for humans.

If an axolotl spends a lot of time in shallow water, its gills will begin to shrink and it will start to use its lungs.

HARSH HABITATS

Amphibians have adapted to survive in places where they normally wouldn't live. Water-holding frogs live in Australian deserts where it's hot and dry for about eight months each year. Their name comes from their ability to store water in their **bladder** or skin for long periods of time. The water can be brought back up to the frog's mouth when it's thirsty.

During the dry season, Australian Aborigines may dig up water-holding frogs. The frogs are gently squeezed until they release some water for the Aborigines to drink. The frogs are then placed back into their burrows.

wood frog

Wood frogs live in the United States and Canada, including in colder areas such as Alaska. They can survive for weeks partly frozen. Their heart and lungs even stop working. Wood frogs produce special substances that lower the freezing temperature of their tissues and protect their cells from damage when freezing. Scientists are studying wood frogs to learn more about freezing human organs for **transplants**.

FRIGHTENING FUNGUS

A type of fungus nicknamed *Bd* has been giving amphibians a deadly disease that thickens their skin. Thick skin makes it hard for amphibians to breathe. The disease has been quickly killing off large populations, really bad news for species that are already endangered.

The *Bd* fungus seems to affect most of Earth's amphibian species, but some seem to resist it. Unfortunately, resistant species, such as the American bullfrog, can still carry the disease and pass it along to other amphibians. Scientists are studying resistant species to learn more about why they aren't affected by the *Bd* fungus. Do they have a special adaptation that protects them? Scientists hope to find out. They're working hard to save amphibians of all kinds and stop more species from dying out.

Between 2010 and 2013, the population of fire salamanders in the Netherlands dropped by 96 percent because of another deadly fungus called *Bsal*.

MORE AMAZING AMPHIBIAN ADAPTATIONS

Frogs and toads use their eyes to help them swallow. When they're eating, their eyes press down inside their mouths to help push food into their throats.

Caecilians don't have ear openings, but a special organ in their ears can detect vibrations.

Chinese giant salamanders are the largest amphibians on Earth. They can grow up to 6 feet (1.8 m) long. They suck prey into their mouth by quickly opening their jaws, and they can go for weeks without eating.

Some glass frogs have see-through undersides. You can see their hearts and other organs. Some even have green bones. This strange camouflage makes it hard for predators to spot them on leaves.

GLOSSARY

adaptation: A change in an animal that helps it stay alive.

bladder: The part of the body that stores urine.

captivity: For an animal, the state of living somewhere controlled by humans—such as in a zoo or an aquarium—instead of in the wild.

endangered: In danger of dying out.

environment: The conditions that surround a living thing and affect the way it lives.

extinct: No longer existing.

habitat: The natural home for plants, animals, and other living things.

nutrient: Food that a living thing needs to live and grow.

opposable: Capable of moving toward and touching the other digits on the same hand, as with human thumbs.

retract: To draw back or pull in.

tentacle: A long, thin body part that sticks out from an animal's head or mouth.

toxin: Harmful poison made by a plant or animal.

transplant: The act of moving something from one place to another.

INDEX

A
Africa, 14
Alaska, 27
Australia, 9, 26
axolotl, 24, 25

B
batrachologist, 9
Borneo, 7
Brazil, 23
bullfrog, American, 28

C
caecilian, 4, 16, 17, 30
camouflage, 5, 20, 40
Canada, 27
Central America, 7

F
frog, 4, 5, 6, 7, 9, 10, 11, 14, 18, 19, 22, 23, 26, 27, 28, 30
frog, banded rubber, 7
frog, hairy, 14, 15
frog, gastric brooding, 23
frog, glass, 30
frog, ornate horned, 22
frog, poison dart (arrow), 10, 11, 18
frog, Vietnamese, mossy, 5
frog, Wallace's flying, 7
frog, water-holding, 26
frog, waxy tree, 7, 19
frog, wood, 27

M
Malaysia, 7
metamorphosis, 6, 24
Mexico, 24

N
neoteny, 24
Netherlands, 29
newt, 4, 12, 13, 15
newt, crested, 4
newt, rough-skinned, 12, 13
newt, Spanish ribbed, 15

S
salamander, 4, 8, 9, 24, 29, 30
salamander, Chinese giant, 30
salamander, dusky, 8
salamander, fire, 29
South America, 7, 20

T
tadpole, 6, 18, 19
tetrodotoxin, 12, 13
toad, 4, 7, 9, 20, 21, 30
toad, Surinam, 20, 21
toxin, 4, 10, 12, 13, 15

U
United States, 27

X
Xenohyla truncata, 23

WEBSITES

Due to the changing nature of Internet links, PowerKids Press has developed an online list of websites related to the subject of this book. This site is updated regularly. Please use this link to access the list: www.powerkidslinks.com/rsa/rsaamph